Is the Spaghetti Ready?

Written by Frank B. Edwards
Illustrated by John Bianchi

Zoo Menu

. . . . . . fruit

. . . . . . bugs

. . . . . . leaves

. . . . grass

. . . french fries

. . . hot dog

. . . spaghetti

. . . pizza

I am hungry.
When can I eat?

Here is your food.
Now go to the table.

We are hungry.
When can we eat?

Here is your food.
Now go to the table.

Here is your food.
Now go to the table.

We are hungry.
When can we eat?

Here is your food.
Now go to the table.

Why are you not eating?

Now we can all eat together.

The End